Put Beginning Readers on the Right Track with
ALL ABOARD READING™

The All Aboard Reading series is especially for beginning readers. Written by noted authors and illustrated in full color, these are books that children really and truly *want* to read—books to excite their imagination, tickle their funny bone, expand their interests, and support their feelings. With five different reading levels, All Aboard Reading lets you choose which books are most appropriate for your children and their growing abilities.

Picture Readers—for Ages 3 to 6
Picture Readers have super-simple texts, with many nouns appearing as rebus pictures. At the end of each book are 24 flash cards—on one side is the rebus picture; on the other side is the written-out word.

Pre-Level 1—for Ages 4 to 6
First Friends, First Readers have a super-simple text starring lovable recurring characters. Each book features two easy stories that will hold the attention of even the youngest reader while promoting an early sense of accomplishment.

Level 1—for Preschool through First-Grade Children
Level 1 books have very few lines per page, very large type, easy words, lots of repetition, and pictures with visual "cues" to help children figure out the words on the page.

Level 2—for First-Grade to Third-Grade Children
Level 2 books are printed in slightly smaller type than Level 1 books. The stories are more complex, but there is still lots of repetition in the text, and many pictures. The sentences are quite simple and are broken up into short lines to make reading easier.

Level 3—for Second-Grade through Third-Grade Children
Level 3 books have considerably longer texts, harder words, and more complicated sentences.

All Aboard for happy reading!

For Katherine Constance,
my living doll—Y.Z.M.

To Nina, Vicky and Hannah.—D.DS.

Text copyright © 2002 by Yona Zeldis McDonough. Illustrations copyright © 2002 by
DyAnne DiSalvo. All rights reserved. Published by Grosset & Dunlap, a division of Penguin
Putnam Books for Young Readers, 345 Hudson Street, New York, NY, 10014. ALL ABOARD
READING and GROSSET & DUNLAP are trademarks of Penguin Putnam Inc. Published
simultaneously in Canada. Printed in the U.S.A.

Library of Congress Cataloging-in-Publication Data is available.

ISBN 0-448-42678-1 (pbk)   A B C D E F G H I J

ISBN 0-448-42836-9 (GB)   A B C D E F G H I J

ALL
ABOARD
READING™
Level 3
Grades 2-3

A Doll Named
DORA ANNE

By Yona Zeldis McDonough
Illustrated by DyAnne DiSalvo

Grosset & Dunlap • New York

4

Chapter One

"Oh Nana, she's beautiful!" breathes Kate.

Nana places the doll in Kate's arms. Kate looks at the doll's china face with its blue eyes, pink cheeks, and small red mouth. The doll's black hair is arranged in a bun. She wears a pretty flowered dress over her cloth body. Boots are painted onto her china feet.

"You've always loved her," Nana says. "Now it's time for her to be yours."

"Thank you!" Kate says. "She's the most beautiful doll I've ever seen. I can't believe she's really mine."

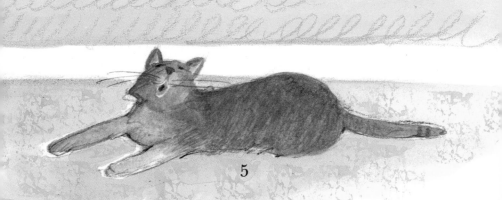

Every year Kate spends a week with her grandmother. It is her favorite part of the summer. For so long, Kate has admired the doll that sits in Nana's china case. Whenever Kate comes to visit, Nana takes the doll out. When Kate leaves, the doll goes back in the case. But not today!

"This doll was made when Abraham Lincoln was president," Nana reminds Kate. "That's almost one hundred fifty years ago. All the girls in our family have gotten her when they turned ten. I know you just turned nine two weeks ago. But I think you're ready now."

"Thank you so much, Nana," says Kate.
Then Kate asks, "Did Mom ever have
the doll?"

"Yes," says Nana, "but she never played
with her much. She didn't like dolls."

"I do!"

"I know!" says Nana, giving Kate a hug. "I loved playing with dolls, too."

Nana gets out an old photo album. She shows Kate a picture of a girl with braids. The girl holds the doll.

"That's me when I first got her," Nana tells Kate.

The rest of the afternoon seems to rush by. Nana gives Kate a trunk full of doll clothes.

"The girls in our family used to make her dresses," explains Nana.

There are white cotton panties. Nana calls them bloomers. There are fancy slips. Nana calls them petticoats. They are trimmed with lace. One dress is made of striped silk. Another is made of faded pink cotton. There is a knitted shawl and a navy cape. They both have tiny moth holes. There is even a velvet muff.

"Maybe I could make her a dress, too,"
says Kate.

"Of course," says Nana. "That's part of
the fun!"

Kate puts the trunk of doll clothes by
her suitcase. It is the last day of her visit.
Kate's mother will be coming soon.

"Nana, there's just one more thing," says Kate.

"What's that, dear?"

"Does she have a name?"

"Oh, she's had so many names." Nana smiles. "I called her Maude."

"That's pretty," Kate says, but she is just being polite. She doesn't really like the name.

"Still, every little girl should name her own doll." Nana says. Kate nods eagerly. "Do you have a name picked out?"

"Dora," says Kate. She thinks Dora sounds pretty and old fashioned—like the doll.

"And she should have a middle name, too," Kate adds. Kate's middle name is Constance, but that doesn't sound right with Dora. "Maybe Anne. Dora Anne."

"Dora Anne it is," says Nana. Then
Nana wraps Dora Anne in a towel and
puts her in a shopping bag. "Now she
won't break on the trip home."

Chapter Two

Riding home in the car, Kate doesn't talk about Dora Anne. She hasn't seen her mother for a whole week, and there is so much to say. Speckles, the cat next door, had kittens. Kate's friend Laurel got a new hairdo. Daddy planted a strawberry patch in the backyard. It is only when they get home that Kate shows her mother the doll.

"The family doll!" Kate's mother says. "She really is pretty, but I never did play with her much."

"Nana told me," Kate says.

"I'm surprised she gave her to you," says Kate's mother. "The family rule always was that you had to be ten."

Kate's mother bites the inside of her lip. Uh-oh. Kate has seen this look before.

"She said I was ready," Kate says.

"That is so nice, honey. Still, I'm a little worried that you may be too young," says Kate's mother uncertainly. "She has to be handled very carefully. She's an antique."

"Mom!" Kate protests. "Nana said!"

"I know how you feel," says her mother gently. "But this doll is so fragile. If she breaks, it would be terrible."

"I promise I'll be careful," Kate says. "Really." She picks up Dora Anne, but somehow the doll slips right through her hands and lands on the floor. Kate can't believe it.

"Oh, no!" Kate cries. She kneels down and quickly looks Dora Anne over. She inspects the doll's china face, hands, and feet for damage. Luckily, there is none.

"She's all right," Kate tells her mother. "Nothing broke."

Kate holds Dora Anne tightly in her arms. "I'm so sorry," she tells the doll. "It won't happen again."

Kate's mother doesn't say anything. There is a long silence.

When Kate speaks again, her voice is very small. "I guess you're right, Mom. Maybe I should wait until I'm ten." She hands Dora Anne to her mother.

"Don't be too sad," her mother says kindly. "I'll take good care of her for you. And she'll be waiting for you on your next birthday."

Chapter Three

Kate's mother doesn't have a china case, so Dora Anne and her trunk are going to be stored on a closet shelf.

Before putting the doll away, Kate measures her. She takes the ruler from her desk drawer. Dora Anne is exactly seventeen inches. She doesn't know why she wants to

know how tall Dora Anne is, but it seems
important.

Kate can't help feeling sad. She was so
excited to get the doll. Now she has to
wait. It's not forever, she tells herself.
Next year she will be old enough. But
right now next year seems very far away.

To take her mind off Dora Anne, Kate decides to organize the other dolls in her room. She has several, though none as special as Dora Anne. Here is the baby doll she used to love. Her name is Tappy. Kate now thinks this is a silly name. And here is the cloth doll with the long blond braids.

All at once, Kate decides she is too old for these dolls. She goes to the laundry room to get the plastic basket her mother uses for the folded clothes.

Into the basket go Tappy and the cloth dolls. Kate adds old puzzles, picture books, and stuffed animals.

She drags the basket into the kitchen.
"What's this?" Kate's mother asks.
"Toys I don't want," says Kate.
"Really?" her mother asks. "Are you
sure?"

"I'm sure," Kate says firmly. "What can we do with them?"

"Daddy and I were thinking about a yard sale," says her mother. She looks into the basket. "We can give the books and puzzles to the children's hospital. You can sell the dolls and keep the money."

"Really?" Kate asks. Her mother nods.

Kate also finds other toys she doesn't want: blocks, more dolls, and games with missing pieces. She throws the games away, but she saves the other things for the sale.

The yard sale is planned for a week from Saturday. Kate uses her markers to make signs. Her friend Laurel helps put the signs around the neighborhood. Maybe Kate can use the money she earns to buy a new doll or toy, but what she would really like to buy is something for Dora Anne.

Chapter Four

It is a rainy day.

"What's this?" Kate asks, holding up a pretty purple box.

"It's the box from my new rain boots," her mother replies.

"Can I have it?"

"Sure, honey," says her mother. "Why?"

"I just need it," Kate says, hurrying off.

Ever since Kate got rid of her old toys, her room has seemed empty. Bare. She wants to fill it up again. But with what? This box just might be the answer.

Back in her room, Kate measures the
box. Twenty inches. It's the perfect size
bed for a seventeen-inch doll, even if the
doll isn't hers. Not yet.

She takes the two pieces of the box
apart. Kate flips over the larger piece to
make the bottom of the bed. Then she
makes four holes in the corners. She fits
straws into each of them. The lid of the
box sits on top. Now it is a canopy! All
she needs are a tiny pillow, sheets, and a
blanket.

Kate runs into her parents' room. "Mom!" she calls. "Do you have any scraps of cloth I could have? Please?"

"Let's see," her mother answers. "I bet I can find something." She goes downstairs. When she comes back, she holds an old dish towel, a couple of cloth napkins, and a pink satin pincushion. The pincushion is shaped like a heart.

"How about these?"

"Great!" says Kate. "Thanks a lot!"

"You've been busy," her mother says. "Will you show me what you're making?"

"Only when it's done," Kate says.

Kate uses the napkins for sheets and the dish towel for the blanket. The pincushion becomes a pillow. Then she proudly carries the bed into the kitchen.

"What a wonderful doll bed!" her mother says. "Look at the pretty canopy. This took a lot of imagination."

"Thanks. I like it, too."

"Which of your dolls will get to sleep in it?" her mother asks.

"Dora Anne, of course," Kate answers. "It's just her size."

"Just her size," says her mother slowly.

"Mom?" asks Kate. "Can I see if Dora Anne fits in the bed? Please? And can Laurel come over to see her? Just for a minute?"

"Of course," says her mother.

Kate calls Laurel, who lives around the corner. She comes right over.

The two girls watch as Kate's mother brings the doll down from the shelf. She brings down the little trunk, too.

"Hello, Dora Anne," Kate says. She carefully places the doll in the bed, tucking the blanket around her.

"She's really special," says Laurel. "I love her eyes. And I love her clothes. Especially the muff."

"Thanks," Kate says. Then she turns to her mother. "Look. The bed is just the right size."

"Yes, it is," her mother agrees.

After the doll is put away, Kate and Laurel sit on the porch. They watch the rain and think of the things they can make for Dora Anne: a table, a footstool, a bench. Laurel promises to save cardboard boxes for Kate.

Chapter Five

The morning of the yard sale is bright and sunny. Kate and her dad help set up. Clothes go by the big elm tree. Books are stacked on the porch. Mom opens a folding table for old china bowls and vases.

"Put your toys on this sheet," Mom tells Kate.

Then they arrange the dolls neatly in a line. Most cost a dollar, but Tappy, the baby doll, costs five dollars. After all, the doll

was once Kate's favorite, and she's still in
good shape.

Soon, people begin arriving.

"How much is this lamp?" asks one man.

"Do you have a fishing pole? Or a bike?"
asks another.

"I'll take these dishes," says a woman.
"Can you wrap them?"

Kate gets bags and makes change. She
sells two dolls for one dollar each.

"Look at this dolly!" says a girl who is younger than Kate. The girl's mother doesn't answer. She carries a baby in a backpack and is looking through the pile of Kate's old clothes.

"Mommy, come see!" the girl calls.

"Sara, you know we can't buy a doll," says the girl's mother. She holds up a dress. "Remember? We need to buy you summer clothes. And your sister, too."

"Please, Mommy," the little girl says. "What if I use my money?"

"That would be all right," her mother says. "How much money do you have?"

"One whole dollar," she says proudly.

"That doll costs five dollars," Kate says quietly.

"Five dollars?" the little girl repeats. "I don't have five dollars. Only one. One dollar." She holds it out.

"Honey, put down the doll and come here," says the woman with the baby. Her voice sounds tired. "I want to see if this dress will fit."

Before putting Tappy down, the little girl hugs her. "She's so pretty," she says sadly.

Kate doesn't say anything, but she has a heavy feeling inside. The little girl's mother walks over with several dresses and a red sweatshirt. Since her dad is helping someone else, Kate finds a bag. Her mother adds up the total.

"Here you are," says Kate's mother. She hands the woman the bag. The woman with the baby and the little girl turn to leave.

"Wait," says Kate. The little girl turns around to see Kate holding out the doll.

"We can't buy that," the woman explains. She takes the little girl's hand.

"She's free," Kate says.

"Free?" says the little girl. "Really and truly?" Her arms close around the doll.

"Really and truly," says Kate, who finds that her bad feeling is gone. Like magic.

"Thank you so much!" says the little girl, hugging Tappy. "She's the best doll ever!"

After the sale is over, Kate counts her money. "Four dollars and fifty cents," she announces.

"That's really good, and it would have been even more if you had sold Tappy instead of giving her away," her mother points out.

"I know," says Kate.

"You were very nice. That little girl had some money," Kate's mother adds. "She could have paid you the dollar."

"I wanted to give it to her," Kate says. "A present."

"Kate, you are a very sweet girl," says her mother. "I'm proud of you."

Chapter Six

That night, Kate falls asleep right away.
Yard sales are hard work, she thinks before
drifting off. The next day is Sunday, so she
gets up late. Lying in bed, she looks over at
the doll bed in the corner.

The bed will be so perfect for Dora Anne.

In fact, it almost looks like Dora Anne
is lying there now. Wait! Kate sits up and
rubs her eyes. She isn't imagining it!
There is a doll in the bed!

She jumps up and rushes across the room.

"Dora Anne! What are you doing here?" she cries, running her fingers over the smooth, pretty face and shiny black hair.

Dora Anne's trunk stands next to Kate's bed and, next to that, a pile of scraps— wool and velvet, checks and dots.

Just then, the door opens a crack. Kate's mother peeks in.

"Good morning, sleepyhead," she says. "I thought I heard you."

"Mom! Dora Anne is in her bed! But why?" Kate says. She looks from the doll's face to her mother. "Didn't you say I wasn't old enough?"

"I was wrong," Kate's mother says, pulling the curtains apart. Morning light fills the room.

"You were able to give up Dora Anne even though you wanted her. You made her that bed. And you gave Tappy to that little girl."

"I knew what she felt like," Kate says.

"Knowing how someone else feels is a big part of growing up," her mother says softly. "You are old enough."

"Thanks, Mom," Kate says, hugging Dora Anne tightly. "Thank you sooooo much!"

She puts her hand on the pile of scraps. "What's this?" she asks.

"The girls in our family made doll clothes," Mom says.

"Nana told me," Kate says. "Did you?"

"No," Kate's mother says, "but now I wish I had. Maybe it's not too late for me to start."

"It's never too late!" Kate says with a smile.

She looks down at Dora Anne. Kate can almost believe that Dora Anne is smiling back.

JÉ   McDonough, Yona
MCD   Zeldis.

     A doll named Dora
     Anne.

$13.89

DATE			